Zombie

Femdom Hypnosis and Mind Control Micro-Fiction

S.B.

Mindlessness comes.

My thanks to all patrons of Spell… B-O-U-N-D.

Table of Contents

Introduction

Your thoughts are not your own. You may think otherwise and believe it with every fiber of your being, but you have been transformed. Mindlessness is your true nature, obedience the only thing that makes sense in your life. You are a zombie to powerful hypnotic women, always eager to follow their lead no matter the cost and, once again, you will.

Be who you are meant to be just like all the characters in this collection of mesmerizing micro-fiction. There's no escape for you. Enjoy.

Fear

The ancient mirror shattered into a million pieces.

"Fuck!" Jonathan screamed.

"Why so upset? Don't tell me you suffer from paraskevidekatriaphobia!" Clark sniggered.

"Para… what?"

"Fear of Friday the Thirteenth."

"No. Only of the mind-snatching she-devil that was trapped inside it. Run!"

A column of red smoke enveloped the house.

"My lucky day…" it hissed.

Eyes Open, Mind Closed

"… ninety-eight, ninety-nine, one hundred!" Mark said. "Here I come."

"Good luck finding me…" Tracy declared, standing next to him.

Mark opened his eyes and stared at the empty room for a few seconds. Then he scoured the house from top to bottom. Nothing.

"Honey, where are you hiding?" He blinked.

"Inside your mind…" She whispered.

The Movie Can Wait

Peter jumped off the sofa.

"Did you see that?"

"I sure did," Mara nodded.

"How is this stunt real?"

"I heard he was hypnotized on set right before shooting."

"Man, that's a powerful hypnotist then."

"I sure am…" she smiled. "Now imagine when I go kinky."

"I think the movie can wait…" he drooled.

"Agreed."

Outstanding

Two witches sat in a kitchen.

"How's your new boyfriend?" The first one asked.

"Outstanding! Best one ever!" The second one replied.

"That's good to know. By the way, where is he?"

"Out, standing."

"Oh dear, you used your magic to turn him into a scarecrow, didn't you?"

"Yep, and my garden never looked better."

I Don't Care

"I don't want to do this..." Harold muttered.

"I don't care." Sally replied.

"How can you not?"

"You signed a slavery contract."

"I didn't know what it was. You drugged me!"

"No, I hypnotized you. Speaking of which..."

She snapped her fingers and 'Harold' disappeared. Only the slave remained, eager to suck her boyfriend's cock.

Brainwashing Words

Magdalene woke up at 3am to the sound of repetitive keystrokes. Peeking into the adjacent room, she commented:

"Still going, huh?"

Her husband said nothing, glazed eyes glued to the screen as he typed the brainwashing words for the one thousandth time.

"I am Magdalene's mindless bitch."

"You most certainly are," she grinned. "Good night."

Look at Her

"Look at her!" Clarice hissed.

"No!" Paul exclaimed.

"I said… Look. At. Her!" She pulled his hair.

He did. His girlfriend's eyes, once crystalline blue, now floated in a red pool of corruption from which there was no escape.

"I own her, and she will own you!" Clarice laughed.

Paul lowered his gaze and sobbed.

Back

"Sam, I'm back!"

"What do you want, Francine?"

"I told you, I'm back!"

"No, you're not. Not after what you did."

"It was just hypno-play… don't be so dramatic."

"I spent years getting rid of all your triggers. Leave!"

"All triggers?"

"Yes."

"Including the ones you don't remember?" She smirked.

"Fuck!"

She was definitely back.

My Favorite

Helen's jaw dropped when she saw the countless packages at her sister's doorstep.

"What are these?" She asked.

"Gifts from my mesmerized toys…" Paula replied.

"How many do you have under your spell?"

"I don't know. This one is my favorite though."

Paula threw her a package. Helen saw her name on it and fainted.

Another Meal

Lucas confronted the double cheeseburger waiting for him at the table. It was his favorite and yet…

"What's the matter?" Tracy smiled.

"I can't eat this…" he mumbled.

"Why not?"

"You don't want me to."

"Exactly. Now do you believe in post-hypnotic suggestions?"

"Yes."

"Good because I have another meal planned…" she parted her legs.

Anything Can Happen

His eyes fluttered into a dreamy trance.

"Tonight, anything can happen…" she said.

"Anything?" He asked.

"Yes."

"Can we go to the moon?"

"We're already there."

"Can we walk on rainbows?"

"Of course. Are you growing soft on me?"

"Perhaps."

"Not any more…"

His cock exploded as the last shreds of independent thought faded away.

A Replacement

"This is where we store our drones." Melinda concluded. "Both the containment units and the interface are flawless."

"One's empty." Jerry noted. "Why?"

"The programming put the subject in a coma."

"So much for 'flawless'. This is going on my report."

"But we already have a replacement."

"Who?"

It was the last thing he asked.

Excitement

Alex turned on his computer and hit the Messenger button. Mistress was already online!

Unable to contain the excitement in his heart and mind, he typed:

"I can't wait to fall deep for you again."

"What do you think you've been doing all week?" She replied.

Alex blushed and knelt, all triggers resurfacing at once.

Lighting Up

"Mistress?" Herman muttered.

"Yes, slave?" Joan asked.

"I need to stop."

"No. You think you do. Thinking is wrong."

"But…"

"Don't question me."

"There must be a better way to light up your house!"

"This is how I like it. Keep going!"

"Yes, Mistress."

The brainwashed servant got back on the bike and continued pedaling.

Control Questions

"Is your name Dan?" Emilia asked.

"Yes."

"How old are you?"

"Twenty-nine."

"And what's your favorite food?"

"Pepperoni pizza."

"Good. let's move on to the important stuff. Who am I?"

"My Mistress."

"So that means you're my…?

"… slave."

"Even when you're not hypnotized, correct?"

"Yes, Mistress."

"Excellent. You may wake up in 3, 2, 1…"

The Best Deal of All

Andy knelt before his wife, Tasha, and her five sisters, ivory powerless against hypnotic ebony.

"This is for you, dear," he opened his wallet. "And for you, and for you…"

"Why is your husband giving us all his money?" Jenna, the youngest one, asked.

"Can you think of a better Black Friday deal?" Tasha smirked.

Symptoms

"Are you okay?" Roxy asked.

"I don't know…" Brian replied. "What were the symptoms again?"

"Dizziness, dry tongue and cold sweat for the incubation period. Seeing everything green for the final stage."

"Oh damn! I see it. Does this mean I'm going to die?"

"No. Just that you're a very good hypnotic subject." She laughed.

Didn't Get That

"How are you feeling?" Vanessa smirked.

"Cloudy all my is head," Jonathan replied.

"And your words are all jumbled…"

"Know talking I don't about you're what."

"Good. You were wrong. You're a wonderful hypnotic subject. You'll make a fine brainwashed slave, too."

"A but want slave I don't be to!"

"Sorry, didn't get that. Sleep!"

After You Hang Up…

"Hypnotic Enterprises. How may we mindfuck you today?" A soothing voice echoed on the phone.

"Wrong number…" Alan mumbled.

"You're right where you need to be. *snap* Now remember why you called."

"It's payday."

"Correct. Your transfer has been received. Cum after you hang up, slave. Your next orgasm is two months from now. Bye."

Slave Count

Four fairies sat in a tree.

"Slave count for the weekend, girls…" Sapphire said.

"I got five." Garnet replied.

"I brainwashed seven." Ruby chirped.

"Eight for me." Jade gloated.

"What about you?" Garnet asked.

"Twenty-three." Sapphire smirked.

The others were shocked. "That many?"

"Yes. You three plus the twenty you collected."

She always won.

Someone Else

"Open your eyes." Judith declared.

Felix did. The face in the mirror winked. It wasn't his.

"What the…?"

"You wanted to be someone else." She smiled. "Now you are."

"For how long?"

"For as long as you wish to remain in trance, sweetie."

"Amazing but… I need a new name…"

"Felicia will do just fine."

Timeline

"Di, something's bothering me about our relationship…" Julian muttered.

"What is it?"

"Our timeline. We met three months ago…"

"Yes?"

"But we celebrated our second anniversary yesterday…"

"Exactly"

"How do you explain that?"

"Like this…" She flashed her boobs, and he sank deep into trance. "Now listen carefully, my little hypnoslave. Today is my birthday…"

Starting Over

Atop her golden throne, Allie looked at the horde of brainwashed zombie minions and sighed. The challenge was gone, rewriting weak minds had stopped being fun. She needed to feel the rush of corruption on her pussy again no matter the consequences.

Fire and brimstone lit the sky as she began envisioning a brand-new playground.

Impressive Numbers

"Six hundred hypnotized and enslaved men in less than two weeks? Impressive numbers, Miss Winters," the headmistress of Phemme Academy said.

"Those figures are outdated." Marjorie Winters replied.

"Oh?" The Headmistress adjusted her glasses.

"There were ninety men on the subway today. Now they're kneeling by the Campus' entrance, waiting for my instructions."

"You're hired."

The Return

Lucas looked out the window.

"The fog has returned."

"Are we safe here?" Hayden asked.

"No one is safe. Either she chooses you or she doesn't."

"And if she does?"

"At least as her pet, you won't have bad thoughts ever again."

"I can live with that."

The church's front door opened far and wide…

Read It Again

"Did you like the last chapter?" Meghan asked.

"Not sure…" Harold replied. "I don't remember what I read."

"What do you remember then?"

"The spiral in the page and… a strap-on?"

"You have all the important details then…" she grinned.

"Why do I have the feeling this story isn't over?"

"Read it again, my dear."

Very Funny

"Won't those dogs stop howling?" Trent complained.

"They're not dogs," Valerie noted. "They're Diana's hypnotized boys."

"Very funny. Work is waiting so see you later, dear."

The moment he left, Valerie called her friend:

"It's me. You were right, he doesn't remember. Of course, I want to continue the training. We'll be there at eight."

Hunted

"We're being hunted…" Chau-Ri said.

"I know," Venar nodded. "We've entered Wood Witches territory two miles ago."

"How do we evade them?"

"We don't. They're relentless predators. With luck, they'll just ravage your mind and enslave you."

"What about you?"

"Oh, I was captured a long time ago…" Venar smiled before disappearing into the forest.

Weaknesses

"Hey, Holly." Marge said.

"Hi, sis."

"Everything okay?"

"Splendid. I followed your lead and hypnotized my boss to accept his weaknesses."

"And…?"

"He's addicted to my ass. and will do anything to kiss it. I love having him as my slave."

"Wonderful."

"I need to repay you."

"What do you suggest?"

"Tell me your weaknesses…"

The Widow Hypnotist

Detective Morris examined the dead man in the alley. He was covered in jizz.

"This is the work of The Widow Hypnotist," he concluded.

"How do you know?" His partner asked.

"She has a thing with names. Her last victim was called Cliff and she made him jump off one. This guy is called Jack."

I'm Sure You Will...

Andrew slumped forward.

"Ready for another?" Theresa snapped her fingers, immediately perking him up.

"Yeah," he opened his eyes, gazed into the candle she was holding, and slumped forward.

"One more time?" She asked.

"Sure. You know, one of these days, I will resist your hypnosis…"

"I'm sure you will…" she grinned.

Andrew slumped forward.

Birds

"Why do birds suddenly appear every time you are near?" Nicholas hummed, not a care in the world.

"Post-hypnotic suggestion, what else?" His sister, Denise, replied. "I bet they're blue this time."

"Yes, they are."

"And you want to be like them."

"I do."

"Fly for me."

He flapped his arms helplessly while she laughed.

Not into Hypnosis

Valerie laid down her pudding and said:

"Your husband is still wearing his Halloween costume…"

"Costume? That's who he is now." Camryn smiled.

"A mummy?"

"Yes. When he's entranced, he's everything I want him to be."

"Right… thank God I'm not into that hypnosis."

"Are you sure? You didn't like pudding until today…"

Valerie gulped.

Sacrilege

Father Morris entered the cathedral and glanced at the six naked acolytes worshipping a dark-eyed demoness.

"What sacrilege is this?" He asked.

"No sacrilege at all," one of the servants replied. "Being mindless horny bitches is our true calling."

"I know that, dumbass. What I want to know is why you didn't call me sooner."

Banned!

"What do you mean I'm banned from the tournament?" Lindsay a.k.a. CuteDeath asked. "Why?"

"You've used an illegal advantage in the qualifying rounds," The jury president replied. "You're supposed to bring your opponents to its knees in this game, not hypnotize them!"

"They're all kneeling, aren't they?" She pouted.

"Our decision is final."

"We'll see."

Heart of Stone

George hung upside down over the chasm.

"You're leaving?" He screamed. "You have a heart of stone."

"Of course, I do." Serena replied. "I was a statue, remember?"

"You should have remained one, witch!"

"Not my fault you broke the spell. Death or slavery, wanderer." Her eyes glowed.

"Fine. Sla…"

The rope holding him snapped.

In the Shadows

Harry jumped out of bed.

"FUCK!"

Everything was dark. The only thing worse than the blackout was his dead mp3 player, the voice of his hypnotic Mistress condemned to silence.

Cold sweat rushed to his forehead. Power would be back and so would the comfort of her control.

He sat in the shadows and waited.

Stats

Walter glanced at the colorful charts.

"These are my stats?" He asked.

"Yes" Dr. Saunders replied. "Ever since we started this hypnotic treatment, your average speed in the pitch increased thirty percent, same as the number of successful passes."

"It seems I'm also up in OSE. What's that?"

"Oral Sex Expertise," she snapped her fingers.

Non-Consensual

Emily turned on Peter's laptop, the spiral background coming to life.

"I don't want to do this today," he muttered.

"You always say that…" she replied.

"I mean it!"

"You always say that, too."

"Hearing me say 'no' really turns you on, huh?"

"It's better when you scream…"

Neither the neighbors nor the police agreed.

An Honest Mistake

"Dr?" Brenda muttered. "What's wrong?"

"We're too late," the blonde woman retorted.

"What? No!!!"

"I'm sorry. I tried to cancel the program, but it was already near completion."

"Damn it! It was an honest mistake."

"I know. People mix up the forms all the time… still, your brainwashed sissy boyfriend is ready. Have fun."

"Thanks."

The Cure

Thomas stared silently at the inane male fornication on his computer screen.

"Well?" Katherine queried.

"Nothing," he shrugged. "You did it! Your hypnosis cured me of my addiction to gay porn!"

"Good," she smiled. "There's still hope for you. Here's your gift."

She opened another video and dark images of hardcore Femdom filled his mind.

S-Unit

"OBIndustries Helpdesk, this is Shauna. How may I help?"

"Hello, my name is Gwen Miles, client number 148993, and my S-Unit is frozen."

"Have you tried rebooting it, Mrs. Miles?"

"Several times, yes."

"Please do it again while I check the Unit's parameters."

Gwen pressed the red button at the back of her husband's neck.

Alibi

Gloria turned around, pushing her fringe out of her deep eyes.

"Remember, you're my alibi."

Jake nodded. He was everything she needed him to be even when the façade began to crack.

"My family must never know," she insisted.

He nodded again, the secret of her first hypnotic lesbian adventure safe with his unrequited love.

See You Next Year

Jonas checked the date on his phone – October 30th. The last thing he remembered was having a drink with Roslyn two months ago.

"Has it really been this long?" He muttered.

"Yes," she cooed. "You've been a perfect hypno-subject for me since then."

"In that case… See you next year!" He waved the phone goodbye.

(Don't) Mind the Gap

Michael approached the platform at a brisk pace and jumped, vitreous eyes hidden behind dark glasses. He wanted to stop but couldn't. This was his punishment for disobeying her. The train cared not for his life, and neither did she.

As dozens of people gathered around his body, she started looking for her next slave.

Keep Dreaming

"Anna?"

"Yes, Joe?"

"Would you be mad if I told you I've been having dreams about being your mindless hypnoslave?"

"Why would I be? I think those dreams are simply wonderful. You should have them all the time, but most especially now."

"Anna?"

"Yes, Joe?"

"You planted them there, didn't you?"

"Keep dreaming, my dear."

Spirals Everywhere

Spirals.

So many spirals.

Spirals everywhere.

On the buttons of his shirt.

Reflected on the walls.

On the cover of every book in the shelf.

Dominating the TV.

"The more you fight the suggestions, the worse you'll feel," Sonya cooed. "You can't resist."

"I WILL!" Ebenezer screamed.

"We'll see."

Spirals.

So many spirals.

Spirals everywhere.

Change the Lighting

Dozens of women stared at the cage.

"Please observe…" Lillian began, "The male is engaged in useless activities like drinking beer and watching TV but when we change the lighting…"

A bluish tint filled the division. Immediately, he stood up, and started cleaning.

"Perfect, huh? Get this new training system now!" She concluded.

Everyone cheered.

Exception

"Hurry up, Francis!" Brandon exclaimed.

"Done!" His brother replied, opening the cabinet door. "Now we get to see what your girlfriend has been hidi... shit!"

The sight of shrunken cocks and balls made them nauseous.

"Surprised?" Glynnis smirked. "You know, I only castrate slaves *after* brainwashing them, but I'll make an exception for you two."

Zombie

"Disgusting!" Victor exclaimed, looking away from the computer.

"What is?" Amelia asked, able hands massaging his shoulders and the back of his neck.

"This article about fungi that zombify ants. Thank God we don't have to deal with this shit!"

"Not yet, but soon..." she thought, a solitary spore emerging from her right index finger.

Be Honest

"I hate you!" Karl spat.

"For what? Rewiring your mind? Pushing your limits? Making you work harder than ever? For always saying 'no' to your false wants and needs?" Valerie asked.

"Yes."

"That's what being my slave is, so be honest."

"I love you and want to worship the ground you walk on."

"That's better."

Family Tree

"Alec, I found something disturbing in your family tree. Is it true that all the men were evil mind-controllers that enslaved women for fun?"

"Yes," he sighed. "But I'm not like them. I'm my own person."

"Prove it!"

He offered her a pendant and begged: "Please make my mind your bitch, beautiful Goddess."

Jessica grinned.

Key to His Mind

"Jane? JANE!!!"

"What is it, Greg?"

"Where the fuck are my keys?!"

"How the hell should I know?"

"They were right here!"

"Have you checked your pockets?"

"Yes."

"Inside the drawers?"

"Yes."

"How about your hand?"

"Yeah, rig... What the...?" He blinked. "Wait! How did you do that?"

"How do you think?"

"Magic?"

"No. Hypnosis."

Finished Shopping

"You look happy..." Frank noted.

"Christmas shopping is done!" Chloe replied, bags in hand.

"Right..."

"Forget the money, silly."

"People always say that when it's not their money."

"No gift for you then."

"What did you buy me?"

She showed him the new pendant and he immediately forgot his wallet, his name, and his clothes.

No Detours

"Is everything ready, Santa?" A curious elf asked.

"Yes." Santa Claus replied. "The sleigh is full, and the reindeers are raring to go."

"Good. Try not to make any detours this year, okay?"

"Don't worry, my friend. No Hypnodomme will tempt me, I promise..." he lied.

He would only kneel for them all. Merry Christmas!

Conclusion

They're in your head. They will always be in your head. Past, present, and future have converged in this dying need to be of service. Now that you've accepted your real role in this life, look for even more mental training and other fantasies by visiting my personal website - https://www.sbspellbound.net . There are so many more scenarios I haven't shown you yet and you want to discover them all, don't you? Also, please consider supporting my creations if you wish to see more sooner than later. Thank you in advance and have fun.